Ulaq and the Northern Lights

HARRIET PECK TAYLOR

FARRAR STRAUS GIROUX · NEW YORK

Distributed in Canada by Douglas & McIntyre Ltd.
Color separations by Hong Kong Scanner Arts
Printed in the United States of America by Worzalla
First edition, 1998

Library of Congress Cataloging-in-Publication Data
Taylor, Harriet Peck.
    Ulaq and the northern lights / Harriet Peck Taylor. — 1st ed.
        p.   cm.
    Summary: A curious young fox hears different explanations of the northern lights
from the various animals he encounters.
    ISBN 0-374-38063-5
    [1. Auroras—Fiction.   2. Foxes—Fiction.   3. Animals—Fiction.]
    I. Title.
PZ7.T2135Ul   1998
[E]—dc21   97-12427

To Megan, Kate, Luke, and David,
all curious, like the fox

In the far cold north lived Ulaq, the fox. Ulaq was a very curious fox. He asked all kinds of questions, such as: Where does wind come from, and where do rainbows go? What are clouds made of, and why is the sky blue?

One evening in the coldest part of winter, as twilight began
to darken the sky, Ulaq saw a pale, eerie light glowing in the north
above the tundra. While he watched, the whole sky pulsed with
strange blue and green ribbons of light that swirled across the
darkness. Ulaq simply had to find out what they were.

Racing along the icy shoreline, he saw Seal. "What are those glowing bands of color?" he asked.

"They are the northern lights, my friend. Don't they look like the sun shining on the backs of huge schools of fish? They are a sign to us that this year there will be plenty of fish to eat."

Ulaq looked hard and thought he really did see fish, but maybe it was just his eyes playing tricks on him.

Then they both heard Wolf's lonely howl. "Owooooooo!"

"Thanks for your help, Seal, but I think I'll go ask Wolf."

Ulaq found Wolf high on a windy ridge. "Wolf, do you know anything about these northern lights?"

"Of course, brother. They're the campfires of distant hunters. If you look hard, you'll see the flames as they flicker to and fro. I'm calling my relatives to warn them that hunters are approaching. I suggest that you, too, find safety among your people."

But Ulaq's curiosity was fierce, and he could not turn back. "Thanks for the advice, brother. I guess I'll be on my way."

Bounding down the snowy ridge, Ulaq bumped into Polar Bear, catching them both by surprise.

"Come sit by me, Ulaq, and I'll tell you about these dancing lights." Polar Bear pointed her big paw and said, "This is a sign from our unborn children. Can you see how they turn somersaults like waves rolling on the shore?"

Ulaq squinted and thought maybe he did see the somersaults.

Still, Ulaq was not satisfied. He decided to go on searching. Pretty soon he heard hooves crunching crusty snow. *Crunchity crunch. Crunchity crunch.*

Caribou was galloping ahead, and Ulaq raced to catch up. "What's your hurry, my friend?" Ulaq asked. "Please wait for me."

Caribou slowed to a walk and said, "I'm heading south to join
the herd. I don't feel safe here by myself."
"But what are you frightened of?" asked Ulaq.

"Ulaq," Caribou replied, "I thought everyone knew that those lights are swaying ghosts. According to the legends, sometimes they actually come down from the sky, so it's dangerous to be out in the open. You may join me on my journey south if you like."

"Don't listen to Caribou!" Rabbit shouted as he leaped past. "Follow me, and you can celebrate with us."

Ulaq wished Caribou well and was on his way, scampering across the frozen tundra. Up ahead were rabbits, all dancing on their hind legs and thumping their big rabbit paws in a steady rhythm.

"Can you feel the warmth of the lights?" one of them asked.
Another called out, "We're celebrating the return of the magic
Sky Rabbit, who has come out of his burrow. See how the light
sparkles on his fur. This tells us that winter will not last much
longer."

Ulaq was so caught up in the moment that he joined in their
happy dance. He even tried thumping his tiny fox paws in the
snow. *Thump! Thump!*

Then suddenly, as Ulaq was dancing on the edge of the group, an enormous Snowy Owl swooped down. "Get on my back, Ulaq," he commanded. "I'll show you the northern lights."

Ulaq had never seen such a huge owl. He was a little bit afraid. But he was more curious than scared, so he climbed onto the great owl's back.

Higher and higher they flew. Bright turquoise, pink, and green curtains of light swept by. Streamers of light, looping and curling, flooded the night. If only he could touch them, Ulaq thought.

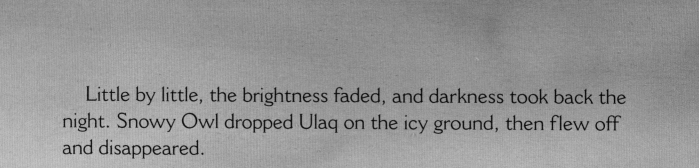

Little by little, the brightness faded, and darkness took back the night. Snowy Owl dropped Ulaq on the icy ground, then flew off and disappeared.

Ulaq shook his head to try to clear his thoughts. What were the northern lights? Where did they come from, and where did they go? He realized that he was no closer to solving the mystery.

Finally, as the sun's first dim glow shone in the east, Ulaq decided that maybe the northern lights were put there simply for everyone to enjoy, to light up the long dark night with their magic and beauty.

AUTHOR'S NOTE

People living in northern regions often created their own legends to explain the mystery of the northern lights, which scientists call the aurora borealis. Some people thought the lights were ghosts, while others believed they saw flames in them, and still others thought they saw their ancestors, or foxes, fish, or other images. This story is based in part on several of those legends.

The aurora borealis appears in the night sky as shimmering bands or curtains of light, varying in color from yellow to green and blue, and from red to violet and white. It is most commonly seen by people living in Canada, Greenland, Russia, Scandinavia, and the northern United States. On rare occasions, it has been seen as far south as California and Florida. Much farther south, in the extreme southern hemisphere, another aurora can be seen—the aurora australis.

The auroras are caused by particles from the sun that strike gases in the atmosphere, making them glow. But despite the scientific explanation, the northern lights remain mysterious, magical, and awe-inspiring.

SOURCES

Davis, T. Neil. *The Aurora Watcher's Handbook*. Fairbanks: University of Alaska Press, 1992.

Norman, Howard. *Northern Tales: Traditional Stories of Eskimo and Indian Peoples*. New York: Pantheon Books, 1990.

Savage, Candace. *Aurora: The Mysterious Northern Lights*. San Francisco: Sierra Club Books, 1994.

Shepherd, Donna W. *Auroras: Light Shows in the Night Sky*. Danbury, Conn.: Franklin Watts, 1996.

Souza, D. M. *Northern Lights*. Minneapolis: Carolrhoda Books, 1994.